Shivers™

GHOSTS OF DEVIL'S MARSH

M. D. Spenser

Plantation, Florida

Published by Paradise Press, Inc. by arrangement with River Publishing, Inc. All right, title and interest to the "SHIVERS" logo and design are owned by River Publishing, Inc. No portion of the "SHIVERS" logo and design may be reproduced in part or whole without prior written permission from River Publishing, Inc. An application for a registered trademark of the "SHIVERS" logo and design is pending with the Federal Patent and Trademark office.

ISBN 1-57657-101-7

30622

EXCLUSIVE DISTRIBUTION BY PARADISE PRESS, INC.

Cover Design by George Paturzo
Cover Illustration by Eddie Roseboom

Printed in the U.S.A.

To David, Rachael, and Abigail

Chapter One

Most people think Bart's Island is a little beach town where families go on vacation to lie in the sun, swim, fish, and take a sailboat out sometimes. Little shops on Main Street sell cool souvenirs like plastic sharks and neon-colored flip-flops.

There's a pier where the locals go fishing and crabbing. You can get ice cream and play Putt-Putt in the park by the boardwalk. You can see real pirates' treasure in the museum and climb all hundred and twenty-nine steps to the top of the lighthouse. I know there are that many, because I counted.

People think it's a quiet little place. But I know the secret of Bart's Island, and I found out the hard way.

I stayed there with my cousins, the Dimswells. Dim is right — at least that's how I felt when Mom told me where I was spending the summer.

"No way," I said.

"Sammy, it'll be lots of fun," Mom said, with that cheery smile she gets when she's trying to convince me of something she doesn't really believe herself.

"But I don't even know them."

"You saw them just a couple of years ago."

"It was six years ago, Mom. How am I supposed to know somebody just because I saw them at Christmas when I was five?"

She knew I was right. But that didn't change anything. The next week I was on a plane flying south.

I knew we didn't have any choice. It's just my mom and me. My dad died when I was little. Right after school let out, Mom got a big promotion at work and had to go to France for two months. She wanted to take me, but knew she wouldn't be around much.

So the logical thing was to send me to the Dimswells. Mom said it would give me a chance stay at the beach, and get to know my dad's side of the family, especially my cousins.

"But Mom," I protested. "They're all *boys*!"

"Boys aren't that bad, Samantha," she said.

"Boys are a nightmare, Mom." My mom just smiled. I hate it when she does that. But there was nothing I could do. I was on my way to the Dimswells.

I knew I was in a weird place as soon as Uncle Tim pulled into the driveway. Their house was two stories, and made of stuff called tabby that's like cement mixed with tiny pieces of shells. It looks neat, but the shells are really sharp.

Uncle Tim and Aunt Sylvie are marine biologists. They work in a lab most of the time. I guess they weren't into house and yard stuff much. The paint was chipping off the shutters and a couple were loose.

The house had a big screened porch with a broken screen door. Two rusty bikes lay across the walkway. The grass looked like it hadn't been cut all spring.

In the yard stood the biggest tree I'd ever seen. It had a huge trunk, with low limbs that stretched across half the lawn. It was covered with gray, mossy stuff that hung in clumps and waved in the breeze.

Uncle Tim saw me looking up.

"They're called live oaks," he said. "Some of the oldest trees around. That stuff hanging down is Spanish moss. Pretty, isn't it?"

It looked creepy to me.

Inside, well — let's just say it looked a lot

different than I was used to at home. Toys lay everywhere, mostly cars, guns, Power Rangers, and Ninja Turtles. The furniture looked weathered, as if it had been climbed on so much that the color had been worn right out of the fabric.

And the noise! It sounded like World War III upstairs with yelling and whoops. I heard a huge thud and a *CRASH*, like a shelf with things on it falling to the floor.

Aunt Sylvie stood at the foot of the stairs hollering, "Hey, you two, cut it out right now, or I'll cream you both."

She saw me and smiled.

"Samantha," she said, opening her arms for a hug. I felt weird looking at her. She looked familiar but I couldn't put my finger on why.

I heard another *WHOOMP, CRRRRASH*, and the tinkling of breaking glass. Aunt Sylvie stormed upstairs.

"All right!" she screamed, "That's *it*!"

Uncle Tim shook his head.

"That's Adam and Andy," he said. "You'll meet them as soon as they escape from time out. Here, let me show you to your room."

He led me upstairs and opened the door to the

4

attic. "It's not fancy," he said, "but I think you'll be comfortable."

Junk lay everywhere. Boxes were stacked on top of each other. Books and magazines had been tossed across the floor. Toys spilled out of laundry baskets — more Power Rangers, Batmen, and G.I. Joes. Legos, Monopoly money and marbles.

In the middle stood a beat-up sofa with a sheet over it. Facing the sofa I saw a TV with video game cartridges and VCR tapes scattered everywhere.

Not fancy, he'd said. No kidding.

Uncle Tim saw the look on my face and laughed.

"It's not exactly the Ritz, but look over here," he said.

I followed him to the back corner where blankets had been hung from the rafters. He pulled one of the blankets to the side.

"Since we don't have any girls, we weren't sure where to put you," he said. "Girls are fussy about their privacy, I hear. Then Sylvie got this idea and, you know, I think she did a pretty good job."

Behind the blanket stood a bed, an old dresser, and a desk with a chair. Just above the bed was a big window.

I touched the quilt that lay across the bed.

"Belonged to your great-grandmother," Uncle Tim said. "She made it, I think. Sylvie will know. Well, you get settled, and then come down and meet the monsters."

I ran my hand along the edge of one of the patches. My great-grandmother. My aunt. My dad. It felt funny to think about these strangers as if they belonged to me.

Chapter Two

"Is *not*!"

"*Is SO!*"

The boys were at it again. I sat right above their bedroom, and I could hear every word through a vent at the foot of my bed. I put my ear to the floor to listen.

"If you do, Adam, I'll tell Mom about the thnake."

"Oh, no, you won't."

"Oh yeth, I will."

"You do and you're dog meat, Andy."

"Watch me."

BAM. A door slammed.

"Booger brain!" *WHAM*, another slam.

I wondered if this was a bad day or if it was like this all the time. Suddenly a boy's face poked from behind the hanging blanket.

"BOO!" he said

I jumped up from the vent, bumping my head on the bed.

"A spy!" the boy shouted. "You're not even here five minutes and I already know you're going to be trouble."

I rubbed my head. "Nice to meet you, too," I said.

"It's not your fault," the boy said. "You can't help it if you're a girl."

"Thanks a lot."

"Girls are just sneaky, that's all. Listening to conversations through vents in the floor is a very girl thing to do."

"Oh, please," I said. "You two were screaming so loud I hardly needed to get on the floor to hear you."

"Yeah? So what were you doing down there, then?"

"Which one are you, anyway?" I asked. "Andy or Adam?"

"So you *were* listening," he said. "I'm Adam. What else did you hear?"

"Nothing," I answered.

Adam was quiet for a minute. "That stuff

about the snake. Andy was just making that up."

"*EEEEEIIKKKKK!*" A scream shot out of the vent. "*Adam Taylor Dimswell!*"

It was Aunt Sylvie, and she sounded really mad.

"I'm going to get that little brat," Adam said, racing for the stairs. I followed, at a safe distance.

Downstairs, in the boys' bedroom, Aunt Sylvie stood by one of the beds. A four-foot black snake slithered on the sheets.

"Gosh, Mom," Adam said, "you see worse stuff at work. What's the big deal?"

"The big deal, young man, is that those animals are behind glass, not in beds, thank you very much. Get it outside, this instant."

"But Rosie *likes* it in here, Mom."

"So help me, Adam, I've had enough of you today. Out! Now!"

"OK, OK," Adam said. Then he noticed Andy sitting on the other bed with a big grin on his face.

"You're dead, creep," Adam muttered.

He scooped up the snake. I felt dizzy just watching the way Rosie wound her way up his arm and across his shoulder. But I was not going to let Adam know that.

9

"Hey, Samantha, ever kissed a real snake?" Adam asked. He shoved the snake at my face. Whatever cool I had disappeared.

"Hey!" I shouted, jumping back.

"Adam, honestly," Aunt Sylvie said, shoving him through the door.

She turned to Andy, who was still smiling. Four of his top teeth were missing. I wondered if he'd lost them naturally, or if Andy had knocked them out.

"You, sir, are still in time out," Aunt Sylvie said, shaking her finger.

"I know," he said, grinning from ear to ear.

"This is Samantha," Aunt Sylvie said.

"I know," Andy said.

"Mr. Andrew, that wasn't very polite. You're supposed to say, 'Hello Samantha.' "

"I know."

Aunt Sylvie cleared her throat and sighed. "This is Andy," she said to me.

"I know," I giggled.

"I see everybody in the family is a comedian," Aunt Sylvie sighed. "Dinner should be ready in half an hour."

A baby started crying in another room.

"And that," Aunt Sylvie said, heading for the

door, "is Alfie."

"He'th two," Andy said. "That meanth I'm not the baby anymore."

"How old are you?" I asked. Andy held up six fingers.

Aunt Sylvie came back into the bedroom with Alfie in her arms.

"It's amazing how the baby sleeps through all this," she said. "Samantha, why don't you give me a hand in the kitchen. Andy, you may come out now, but no more roughhousing — you hear me?"

"Yeth, ma'am," Andy said.

At dinner, the whole crew assembled around the huge kitchen table. I got to meet Allen, the oldest, who was fifteen. He worked at Dennis's Super-Duper Ice Cream Extravaganza on Main Street down by the pier.

Cool. That meant freebies.

I sat across from Adam and Andy. Why they weren't separated, I don't know. They kept sneaking pieces of chewed up food onto each other's plates. Disgusting.

Most of the boys looked like Uncle Tim, with reddish hair and long legs.

But Adam was different.

11

He was my age, but shorter. He had straight brown hair with spiky bangs that fell into his face. His eyes were like Aunt Sylvie's — almond shaped, and turned up at the outside, like a cat's.

Then it hit me. He looked like Peter Pan! Funny. That's what my mom used to say about me back when my hair was really short.

Adam speared a piece of hot dog with his fork.

"Beanie Weenies. My favorite!" he said. "Hey Samantha, know why beans are a specialty on Bart's Island?"

"Adam," his mother warned.

"Cause on Bart, we love to fa- . . . "

"That's quite enough, thank you," Uncle Tim interrupted.

The boys were excused and they ran outside. Aunt Sylvie took the baby upstairs for a bath. I helped Uncle Tim clear the table. Then he sat down to read the paper.

For the first time, it was quiet in the house, and I got this weird feeling in the pit of my stomach. It moved up my body like a shiver, into my chest and my throat. I thought I might throw up and cry at the same time.

Then I realized I missed my mom. No wonder

they call it being homesick.

Uncle Time looked up from his paper. "You OK?"

I nodded, afraid that if I opened my mouth, my dinner might spill out.

"Been down to the beach yet?"

I shook my head.

"Then what are you doing staring at me, silly girl? The world is out there," he said, waving toward the door. "No kids allowed inside until sunset. House rules."

I stood on the porch and looked around. Across the street were more houses. Beyond them lay the ocean. A wide path was marked with a sign that read: PUBLIC BEACH ACCESS.

Mom would never have let me walk around a strange place by myself, or told me to come home when it got dark. I crossed the street and headed for the beach.

I'd been to beaches before. But they weren't like this.

I was used to calm, blue water and snow white sand. Here, the water was a gray-green with wild, foamy waves. The sand was gray too, like the skin of a wet seal.

Layers of heavy gray clouds covered the sky.

I felt so sad I started to cry. I just wished I could talk to my mom. But she was on a plane somewhere, going very far away.

A flock of seagulls flew overhead. There must have been a hundred of them. They made a huge commotion, squawking and screaming to each other.

With all that noise, and the pounding of the waves and me crying, it's no wonder I never heard my captors until they were on top of me.

Chapter Three

"Quick, Sergeant Andrew, surround the Alien!" the voice said.

I looked up to see two huge Super Soakers pointed in my face.

"We've got her captured, Commander, thir."

"You know, Sergeant, this alien is even uglier than the last one. I think we'll have to kill it."

"Yes, thir. Kill it."

"Adam, don't you dare . . . "

"Ready. Aim . . . "

I broke away and ran, with the boys in hot pursuit. I felt a cold wet splash on my back. Then another on my leg.

Adam tackled me, and we fell to the ground. Sand flew into my mouth. He and Andy took my arms and pulled me toward the water.

"How about a swim, Samantha?" Adam asked.

"Let me go!" I hollered.

I kicked and twisted. We fell in a heap in the sand. A wave washed over us.

"Jerks!" I screamed. Salt water had gone up my nose, and I was wet and sandy all the way to my underwear. The boys shook the water from their hair and laughed.

I hate to admit it, but I started to cry. Right in front of the boys. And I was so mad at myself, it made me cry even harder.

I staggered to my feet and ran back toward the house. My sneakers were wet and heavy, and it was hard to go very fast in the sand. Adam caught up to me.

"Hey, Samantha. Don't be such a baby," he said. "We were only kidding around."

"Shut up, jerk," I said. "And it's not Samantha, for your information. It's Sammy. Now leave me alone."

I wiped my tears with the back of my hand. Suddenly, I felt a terrible stinging. I'd rubbed sand right into my eyes. It felt like my eyes were on fire. I couldn't open them. I couldn't see!

"Ow!" I yelled. "Sand in my eyes! Get it out!"

"Come on," Adam said. He shoved my head under a spigot that stuck out of the ground. The water poured out fast and cold.

I bent over and tried to open my eyes to let the water flush out the sand. It burned like anything, but it worked. I sat up and rubbed my eye.

"Don't do that," Adam said. "You'll scratch the cornea."

"What'th a cornea?" Andy asked.

"It's part of your eyeball," Adam said.

I tried to open my eyes. I felt wet, soggy, sandy and miserably.

"This is all your fault," I said, looking at both of them.

"You know something?" Adam said, "You'd be a lot more fun if you didn't act like such a girl."

I started walking back to the house. I'd had enough.

"Hey, Thammy," Andy said, running up beside me. "Want to go ghotht hunting?"

"What?" I asked. I had trouble understanding him, with that lisp of his.

"Samantha does not want to look for ghosts," Adam said. "Girls are too wimpy for that stuff."

"It's *Sammy*, and we are not," I shot back.

"Thee, Adam? I told you she'd go. Let'th go! Pleath!"

17

"Go where?" I asked. "What ghosts?"

I eyed Adam carefully. I wasn't in the mood for any more of his tricks, but one thing I loved more than anything was ghosts — or at least ghost stories.

"Nah, forget it," Adam said. "It's too late."

"No it's not. Pleath. Let's show Thammy the graveyard," Andy said, tugging on Adam's arm.

"Quit it, runtski," he said.

"Adam'th a thcaredy cat!"

"Am not! It's fixing to rain, and it's late."

As if on cue, lightning crackled across the sky, followed by a loud clap of thunder.

"See?" Adam said. "Come on, let's go home."

Andy turned to me and whispered loudly enough for Adam to hear, "He's thcared he'll thee the ghotht again."

"You saw a ghost?" I asked. "A real one?"

"It was nothing," Adam said.

"Nuh-uh!" Andy said. "It wath real and . . . "

"I said forget it, OK?" Adam said. He stormed up the path, leaving us behind.

"I'm telling the truth. Honetht," Andy said. "Adam thaw a ghotht. It wath calling hith name. He even cried."

Another bolt of lightning flashed across the

sky. The air boomed with thunder. The sky turned from gray to black. Any second, it was going to pour.

"Come on, Andy, let's talk about this back at the house," I said.

The wind whipped around us. Sand stung our arms and legs. My hair flew everywhere, and I had trouble seeing.

"Follow me," Andy called.

We walked up the path between the sand dunes. But we weren't fast enough. The rain fell as hard as if someone had turned on a hose. I'd never seen rain come on so fast.

Then, when we were almost at the street, we heard . . . *CRAAAACCKKK!!*

Chapter Four

"Andy!" I screamed.

Lightning shot down the sky, hitting a tree that stood beside the path. A jolt of electricity shot up from the ground, through the roots. The whole tree lit up electric blue.

BOOOMM! The thunder shook the air like a bomb, and knocked me off my feet. For a second, I thought I'd been hit by lightning, too.

The tree split right down the middle. Curls of smoke rose from the center. The hairs on my arm stood straight up, and my ears rang.

Andy ran over to me.

"Thammy?" he asked. "Are you OK?"

My head was spinning, but I managed to get to my feet. I was terrified.

We ran across the street and onto the front porch. My ears still rang. My heart pounded in my chest, and I felt tingly all over.

Aunt Sylvie, Uncle Tim, and Adam came flying onto the porch.

"Good Lord!" said Aunt Sylvie. "Are you two all right?"

Andy and I nodded. The smell of burning wood hung in the air. Aunt Sylvie, Uncle Tim, and Adam peered through the sheets of rain at the smoldering tree.

"Good Lord," Aunt Sylvie said again.

She ushered us all inside, then called the doctor, "just in case." He told her to keep an eye on me, and if my ears didn't stop ringing by morning, to bring me in to see him.

Exhausted, I said my goodnights and went up to the attic. Adam followed me.

I went into my so-called room, behind the blankets. Adam plunked himself down on the sofa and started to play video games.

I wished he would leave me alone. I wished he would go to bed. I peeled off my wet clothes and put on my big Grateful Dead T-shirt.

"Cool," Adam said, holding up a corner of the blanket. "You like the Dead?"

"Can't you knock?"

"How am I supposed to knock on a blanket?"

"Maybe you could just say it. Like, you know — knock, knock."

"Who's there?"

"Very funny."

"Very Funny Who?"

I rolled my eyes. "Is there something you want," I asked impatiently.

"As a matter of fact, there is," he said.

"And?"

"Well, ummmm," he said. "Oh, never mind," he said finally, and got up to leave.

"Wait, Adam," I said. "Tell me."

"Forget it. I changed my mind."

"OK fine," I said. I wanted to go to bed.

"All right," he said. "I'll tell you. But you have to promise not to tell a soul. I know that's hard for girls. To keep secrets and all."

"I'm going to murder you in about one second."

"First, you need to blood swear."

"Oh, please," I said. "I am not about to cut my finger just so you can tell me some dumb story."

"It's about the ghost, Samantha," Adam said.

He went over to some boxes stacked in the corner, pulled out his mother's sewing box and came

22

back with a needle. He jabbed it into the tip of his finger. A drop of blood appeared.

"Now you," he said, handing me the needle.

"You're nuts," I said.

"Or else I'm not telling you a thing," he said.

Thinking he was probably one of the weirdest kids I'd ever met, I took the needle and held it above my finger.

"I can't do this," I said finally.

"Sure you can," he said. "Here, hold your finger like this."

He held my finger and quickly pricked it with the needle. I jumped back.

"Hey, that hurt!" I said.

"Poor baby," he said.

He held his finger up. I placed mine on his and we pressed them together, making sure we mixed the blood.

Adam got a wild look in his eye. He was sort of scaring me. Looking back on it later, I wished I had never made that blood pact with him.

I wished I had never heard what he told me that night.

Chapter Five

"So what about the ghost?" I asked.

We were sitting on the bed.

Adam leaned over and opened the window. Outside, the rain fell and the wind howled. The trees creaked and whined. In the distance I heard a clanging sound.

"What's that noise?" I asked.

"The ropes from the sailboats hitting the masts," Adam said, with a wicked smile. "A good night for a ghost story, eh?"

"Let's get on with it," I said. I was starting to feel uneasy.

He pointed out the window. "Tell me what you see," he said.

"Nothing," I said. It was as dark a night as I've ever seen.

"Out there," Adam said, "out past where you can't see, is the marsh. Devil's Marsh."

24

"Yeah, so . . . "

"It's called Devil's Marsh because, for hundreds of years, people who have been careless enough to go into the marsh have never come out alive."

I shrugged.

"Do you know what a marsh is?" Adam asked. "It looks like a huge meadow of tall grass, but really there's no solid ground. People who don't know better think it's safe. But below the grass, it's all water and mud. If you go in there, it will suck you down to a muddy grave, like quicksand. If the alligators and snakes don't get you first."

"Alligators?" I asked, looking out the window.

Ghosts were one thing. Alligators were another.

"Yeah," Adam said. "Sometimes they come out of the marsh, especially when they're hungry. A few years ago, an alligator got into someone's back yard and ate a baby. Right in front of his mother. They said it happened so fast, the baby's feet were still kicking as they went down."

Adam wiggled his fingers back and forth to show me.

"Oh, shut up," I said. "That's the stupidest thing I ever heard."

"I swear it's true."

"So what about the *ghost*?" I said. I was beginning to feel I'd pricked my finger for nothing.

"Some of the people who died in Devil's Marsh haunt the island to this day," he said. "Ask anyone who lives here. They'll tell you lots of stories."

He rubbed his hands together, his eyes glowed, and I could see he was going to tell me one himself.

"A long time ago, there used to be a small farm on the other side of the marsh," he said. "One day, the farmer's daughter forgot to lock the gate, and their only hog got loose and went into the marsh. The farmer was furious. They needed that hog for food for the winter. The daughter felt terrible. She was afraid her family would starve. So she went in after the hog, and never came out. The farmer was so filled with grief he shot himself in the head."

I put my hand to my mouth, horrified.

"Now, sometimes at night, you can hear this high pitched squealing, like a stuck pig," Adam continued. "But there *are* no pigs around here any more. When the fog rolls in and the marsh gets misty, people say they've seen the ghosts of the farmer and his daughter floating above the grass. You can hear the little girl wailing. And gunshots, too."

"You've heard it?" I asked.

"Plenty of times," Adam said, and shivered.

"What did Andy mean when he said you'd seen a ghost?"

Adam looked at his shoes.

"I was getting there," he said. " I just want you to understand that I'm not crazy. Lots of people have seen stuff."

"And?"

"OK," Adam said. He took a deep breath. "One night I sneaked out of the house to go crabbing on the pier with some guys who live on the other side of the island. It was like three in the morning, and a storm started to blow in. Really fast, like it did today. We knew we had to get home, or we'd get caught in it. So, I'm on my bike, in the dark, with the wind and thunder. Just as I was coming around the bend along side the marsh — *BANG!* — lightning hit a tree right as I passed it. Same as you. Threw me off my bike."

"Did the tree go blue?" I asked, amazed.

"I didn't really see anything, it was so fast," he said. "Just this huge flash of light and then — *BANG!*— this mondo explosion! So there I am on the ground, and I'm all tingly and my ears are ringing like crazy. I'm not sure if I've been hit. Then I smell something burning, and I can just make out the tree, with smoke coming out of the middle."

"That's what happened today, too," I said.

"So I got back on my bike and rode home. I never told anybody about the lightning because then I'd catch it for being out. I slept forever. When I finally woke up, the tingling was gone, but I still felt weird. Like the insides of my body were rearranged."

"I know!" I said. "Me too!"

Lightning sizzled through the sky. Adam started counting. At eleven, we heard a thunderclap.

"Eleven miles," he said. "It's moving out."

"So," I said. "What about the ghost?"

"I'm getting to that," he said.

He stared out the window, as if he were seeing something that I could not:

"After dinner that next day, I was feeling a little crazy," he said. "I had to get out. I rode back to the marsh to check out the tree. It was charred black along one side, and a big branch was broken and leaning toward the ground. It smelled kind of sickly sweet. I felt like I was going to blow chunks if I didn't get out of there."

I nodded, still waiting for the part about the ghost.

"I was getting on my bike to leave," Adam said, "when I heard someone — or, should I say, some*thing* — call my name. Twice. Only, it was so quiet. I wasn't sure if I'd really heard it. But then it came again."

His eyes grew large. He looked scared just by the memory.

" 'Adam, Adam,' " he whispered in a ghostly voice. "That's what I heard. I thought I was going crazy. I figured my ears still weren't right, or maybe it was the wind."

His voice dropped to a whisper again.

"Then I heard it some more," he breathed. "It called, 'Adam, you can hear me now, can't you, Adam?' "

He shivered again. I stared at him.

"Then whatever it was told me that now, because of the lightning, I could hear and see stuff other people could not," he continued. "It said something about being changed so I could experience *their* dimension. I didn't hear this part with my ears, but inside my head. Like it was speaking directly into my brain."

"No way!" I said. "Get out!"

"Samantha, I swear I'm telling the truth,"

Adam said.

"So then what?"

"Well, it looked like smoke was coming out of the trunk again — only I realized it wouldn't still be burning a whole day later. Suddenly the smoke turned into the shape of a head. It had with eyes like bottomless pits. And a huge, gaping mouth! And it made this horrible, ear-splitting, shrieking sound — like this, '*EEEEEEEEEIIOOOOOOOO!*' "

"Stop," I said, covering my ears.

Adam pulled my hands down.

"The worst part," he said. "was when it opened its mouth these *things* flew out!"

"What do you mean, *things*?"

"Like teeny gremlins or goblins or something. They flew out of its mouth like moths and swarmed around my face. I swatted, but my hands went right through them! They had wings like bats, and long bony fingers with sharp claws, and snaky tails. Their faces looked like foxes, with pointy ears and long snouts and sharp little teeth. They flew around my head, and I felt them in my hair. They tried to crawl into my ears."

Adam reached over and tickled my ear.

"Quit it!" I said, pushing his hand away. He

was grossing me out.

"I got on my bike and pedaled as fast as I could. I was totally freaked. I wanted to tell Mom and Dad, but I knew they wouldn't believe me. So I told Allen. He said I was nuts. So then I told Andy. Who, of course, bought the whole thing."

I looked at Adam. I was ready to believe him, but I didn't want to be just as gullible as his little brother, who was only six.

"Did you just make all that up?" I asked.

"What do you think?" he said. He looked at me with that sneaky smile of his.

"I'm going to kill you!" I yelled, throwing my pillow at him. "Get out of my room! Get out! I really hate you."

"Hey, Sammy, be careful now," Adam said. "If it happened to me, it can happen to you. You're touched now, too."

He pointed at my head and made an electric noise: "ZZZZZ. ZZZZ."

"Out!"

Adam laughed an evil little laugh and ran downstairs.

I was boiling mad. My friends all tell me I'm too quick to believe stuff, and they're always playing jokes on me. I looked down at my finger. It was still sore.

That Adam Dimswell! I vowed I would get him back. Somehow. Someday.

Chapter Six

The next morning, I was eating breakfast with Aunt Sylvie and Alfie when Adam The Creep sneaked up behind me.

"*ZZZZZ. ZZZZZ,*" he buzzed.

"Quit it!" I hollered. He and Andy rolled on the floor, hysterical.

"Adam, Andy, stop teasing your cousin," Aunt Sylvie said, stepping over them to get Alfie, who was in the highchair lobbing Cheerios at me. "Get up and eat, this minute."

Boy, it was going to be a long summer. It looked as if Adam had told Andy about last night. Great. Now I had a six-year-old thinking I was a butt-head, too.

"How are you feeling this morning, Samantha?" Aunt Sylvie asked. "Your ears feel OK?"

"What'd ya say, Mom?" Adam bellowed, his hand cupped to his ear.

Andy giggled so hard he fell off his seat again.

"I'm fine, thank you," I said.

"Fie, tank oo," Alfie said, mimicking me. He flicked a Cheerio from his highchair. It landed with a plop right in my bowl.

Adam and Andy lost it. Even Aunt Sylvie couldn't stop them, and eventually we were all laughing.

On weekdays, Uncle Tim left for work before anyone else was up. Aunt Sylvie fed the boys and took Alfie to the daycare center. Allen was supposed to watch Adam, Andy, and now me, until Uncle Tim got home. But Allen didn't get up until lunch time. Then he spent most of the day watching TV before leaving late in the day for the ice cream shop.

That meant Adam, Andy, and I did pretty much what we wanted during the day.

I wondered if my mom would have been OK with that. Even though I was ten, and would soon be baby-sitting other kids, she was still getting baby-sitters for me. I'd never been allowed to just run around with my friends.

Maybe it was because the Dimswells lived in a small town, but it was nothing for Adam and Andy to ride their bikes by themselves down to the pier, or to

Main Street, or to the beach.

I wasn't crazy about being stuck with them all the time. But I liked the idea of being able to go where we wanted. Uncle Tim had rented a bike for me, and we spent most of the day riding around.

Late that afternoon, we rode to Dennis's Super-Duper Ice Cream Extravaganza on Main Street. Denny, the owner, gave us free gummy worms. I thought they were horrible, but Adam and Andy loved them.

Adam stuffed as many in his mouth as he could. Some were hanging out. Then he chewed them with his mouth open.

"Hey Sammy, look," he said.

"Disgusting," I said.

"Yeah, dithgusting," Andy said. "Let me try."

"Dis-gus-ting," Adam sang in a prissy voice. I swatted him. He laughed, jumped on his bike, and sped off.

"Hey," Andy yelled. "Wait up!" Then he was gone, too.

Afraid I'd get lost if I didn't follow, I rode after them, trying hard to catch up.

Chapter Seven

Keeping up with Andy and Adam wasn't easy.

They zipped through parking lots and down alleys. They would disappear around corners and, when I rounded the curve, they were gone. Then they'd dart from behind a house or a tree, and I'd peddle like crazy to catch up.

They were doing it on purpose. I could tell.

That's what happened when we rode past the lighthouse. At the stop sign, I took a minute to look up at the lighthouse, and when I looked back at the street they were gone.

I had no idea which way to go.

"Hey, guys!" I called out.

There was no reply. Darn those boys, I thought. I was getting tired of their tricks.

"Adam? Andy?"

Still nothing.

I looked to the right. Along the street were

some beach houses and then the dunes. I figured they couldn't have gotten their bikes over the dunes that quickly.

"Guys?" I called again.

I heard only the cries of the seagulls and the distant rumble of the surf.

The road ahead was lined with more houses. Then it dead-ended at the dunes, too.

To the left, the road continued for quite a distance. I saw houses, a bank, and a church.

"Hey, Adam! Andy! Where are you?" I called.

By now, I really didn't expect them to answer. Either they were hiding or they were long gone.

I took a deep breath and turned left.

I pedaled slowly, looking carefully at the buildings and the huge live oaks that lined the street. I expected the boys to jump out at me any second.

I reached the end of the block, and still saw no trace of them.

Again, I looked to the right. To the left. Straight.

The roads were laid out like a grid. Each had more houses, more trees. There was no telling which way they had gone. By now, I was getting scared. And angry too.

"This isn't funny!" I yelled, hoping I'd hear Andy giggle from wherever they were hiding.

I tried to remember how we had come to Main Street, but all the streets looked the same.

I decided to go straight for another block. I came to the elementary school I'd seen on my drive in with Uncle Tim. Now we're getting somewhere, I thought.

I pedaled faster, sure I was on the right track back to the house. I flew past the school, past a gas station, past more houses. Gradually, the houses got further apart, and then I passed a funny little shack with a hand painted sign out front that read: LIVE CRABS. SPELLS CAST. CHEAP.

That's an idea, I thought. A nasty little spell might be just the thing to get back at Adam The Creep Dimswell. I wondered what sort of curse I could put on him. Blistering tongue? Pus under the toenails?

Just then I heard someone call my name.

I slammed on my brakes and whipped the bike around.

"Adam, you are in big trouble!" I shouted.

But it wasn't Adam who stood behind me. Not even close.

<u>Chapter Eight</u>

How I wished it was Adam waiting for me. As mad as I was at him, I would have preferred that.

Standing beside me was an old woman with skin as dark and soft as leather.

"Honey," she said.

Honey? Had I heard wrong? I was sure she'd said Sammy.

I looked at her closely. She was tiny — not much taller than I was. She had gray hair piled up on top of her head and she wore a long, colorful caftan. She was barefoot, with rings on her toes. She smelled like sour milk.

Around her neck hung dozens of necklaces, made of gold, silver, and all sorts of beads. One was adorned with things that looked like alligator teeth.

She pointed a shaky finger at me. Her nails were painted orange.

"The power," she said. "You got the power."

Her eyes were hazy and sort of yellow. She only had three teeth that I could see — two on the top and one on the bottom.

"You got the power, honey. You got the devil's power. For sure."

"Excuse me?" I said.

"I see it all around you," she said, waving her arms. "You be a touched one. I see it with these blind eyes. You got the power. *Take it*," she hissed like a snake. "*Take it.*"

I put my feet to the pedals and sped away as fast as I could. Great, I thought. Not only am I lost, not only was I almost killed by lightning, not only do I have to deal with the two most irritating boys on this planet — but now I have been accosted by a witch.

That was it. I was calling Mom — and she would either come home or take me to France with her. But I was not spending one more day in this place.

I pedaled and pedaled. I didn't care which direction I rode. I flew past a few more houses, and then it was mostly trees.

They lined both sides of the street, and their branches came together overhead, forming a canopy of leaves and wispy Spanish moss. Patches of sunlight shone through. Ahead, everything looked like a jungle.

I was going deeper into the island, away from the beach. And the Dimswells lived near the beach.

Wait, Sammy, I thought. You're going to make this worse. Stop.

I hit the brakes. Maybe I should turn around, I thought. Only this time, I'd go around the witch's shack. Then I could go to a gas station and call. It was a good plan.

I was about to turn around when the most amazing bird I've ever seen flew right over my head. It looked like a parrot, only smaller, with emerald green feathers and red, yellow and blue on its wings. It flew into the bushes along the road.

I dropped my bike and walked over to it.

The bird cocked its head to one side and blinked at me. Then it flew off. I watched it dip past the thick branches of the tree and land on . . . a tombstone?

Just past a bank of ferns lay an old graveyard. It was surrounded by a black iron fence with pointy spikes, but the gate was open.

I love graveyards. I like to read the tombstones and see who is buried where, and when they died. This must have been the one Andy was talking about.

I thought about the witch, and about Adam's stupid ghost stories.

Maybe I shouldn't be here, I thought.

Then I looked at the bird. He blinked at me again, as if he was inviting me in.

Oh, what the heck, Sammy, I thought. You've been to graveyards before. I stepped inside the gate, and walked over to the bird. This time, he didn't fly away.

I read the tombstone: *Martha Bay Parker. Beloved Wife and Mother. March 18, 1791 to August 15, 1846.*

These were really old!

The bird flew to another tombstone. I followed it. It seemed as if he was picking the ones he wanted me to see.

I ran my fingers over the weathered letters: *Winslow Thomas Stephens. December 21, 1760 - April 3, 1776. No braver son died for this country.*

Cool! He must have fought in the Revolutionary War, I thought. He was only fifteen when he died. It gave me the willies to think about it. That's how old Allen was!

The bird took off again. This time he flew to the other side of the graveyard, landing on a high wall.

When I got closer, I realized it was that tabby stuff the Dimswells' house was made of.

There was an arched opening in the wall, and it surrounded what looked like a family plot. Vines and weeds had grown over some of the tombstones.

There were six big stones, and four little ones. Really little ones, for babies.

Eeoww. That was creepy.

I stepped back outside to see if the family name was on the wall. I saw it carved across the top of the arch in fancy letters.

McMillan.

Oh, man! I freaked. My heart started beating so fast I could barely breathe.

McMillan.

That was *my* last name! This was *my* family plot!

Chapter Nine

I tried to calm myself down. I breathed in through my nose and out through my mouth like my mom taught me to do whenever I got freaked.

I really didn't know anything about my dad's family. He died when I was just a baby. Mom never talked about it much. I went to my dad's grave once, but it made Mom cry and we never went back.

Dad's graveyard was quiet and neat, with rolling lawns and a few trees. It felt lonely, maybe, but not creepy like this place. It felt really weird to look at these tombstones, knowing I was related to the bones under the ground.

The next one read: *Hattie Smith McMillan. January 22, 1889 to January 11, 1969.*

I wondered who she was to me — a great-great-grandmother, maybe. Suddenly, I did not feel scared anymore. Aunt Sylvie would know who these people were.

This was so exciting! I looked at another: *Nathaniel Mason McMillan. July 15, 1886 to May 1, 1969. A loving father to us all.*

Maybe he was Hattie's husband, my great-grand-whatever.

There were others: *Jonathan Heller McMillan, Elizabeth Brody McMillan, Mary Ann McMillan.*

I looked at the baby tombstones. They were blank, except for one that read: *Lil' Bit. We will miss you.*

The last tombstone was in the back corner, and it looked newer than the others. It was covered with carvings of angels and doves and stuff like that.

Samantha Lewis McMillan. May, 9 1906 to August 22, 1987.

Now I *really* couldn't breathe. Samantha Lewis McMillan! That's me! I mean, that's my name. And she died on my birthday!

I felt dizzy. Shivers ran up my spine. I reached out to steady myself. My hand knocked the top of the tombstone. A little angle fell off, hit the marble slab below, and shattered.

Now I've done it, I thought.

I picked up some of the pieces and looked at the base where it had broken off. It seemed like it had been broken already, and someone had just put it back without really fixing it. But now the head had broken off and the wings were all over the place.

I picked up another piece. The angel had been holding a heart. It was still in one piece, but it had a crack down the middle.

I put the heart in my pocket and swept the rest of the mess into the grass.

I pedaled back toward town as fast as I could. At least, I *thought* I was going in the right direction, but I didn't start to see houses like I should have. Just more trees.

I started feeling panicky. I was really lost. It was surely dinnertime by now.

The trees stopped, and a wide field opened up in front of me. It seemed to go on for miles. Off in the distance, on the other side, I saw houses.

I was at Devil's Marsh! And the Dimswells' house was on the other side.

I stopped and caught my breath. Off in the distance I heard rumbling.

Oh, no. It couldn't be.

Sure enough, storm clouds, thick and black,

began rolling in. They swept over the island like a huge blanket. I prayed I could make it to the house before the storm hit. I had no interest in trying my luck with lightning again.

The wind picked up. The marsh grasses whipped around wildly.

Out of the corner of my eye, I saw a white flash.

Then I saw it again.

It was rising up out of the grass. And coming right at me.

Chapter Ten

"*EEEEUUUWW!*" it screeched.

The cry cut through me like a knife. A huge cloak of white rose up in front of me.

I screamed and shut my eyes. The ghosts! Adam had been telling the truth!

"*EEEUUUWW! EEEUUWW!*"

I felt a fluttering all around me. I covered my head with my arms. They surrounded me. I felt their stale breath all over my skin. This was it. I was a goner.

Then, suddenly, nothing. It was quiet.

I opened my eyes just in time to see two huge white birds fly over my head.

"*EEEUUUWW!*" they called to each other.

Herons.

Not ghosts, Sammy. Herons. Big birds that live in the marsh. Get a grip.

BOOM! The thunder crashed again.

I had no time to lose. I couldn't go back the other way now. It was Devil's Marsh or nothing. Ghosts or no ghosts.

I got back on my bike and pedaled as fast as I could. The road turned and cut straight through the middle of the marsh. I could see where they built it up with dirt and rocks to keep it above the water.

The further into the marsh I rode, the harder it was to pedal. The wind was strong, and I rode straight into it. It felt like a big hand holding me back.

The thunder boomed closer. The sky grew so dark it looked like nighttime.

I realized I was on a narrow bridge. Underneath, creeks twisted and turned through the tall grass. I rode onto the road again, with the marsh to either side.

That's when I noticed it looming ahead of me. The tree.

The tree in Adam's story. It was split down the middle. One half struggled to stay alive, sprouting a couple of branches and a few stray leaves. The other half was black as ink.

OK, I thought, just because there's really a tree doesn't mean the rest of the story is true.

Rain started to fall. A thick curtain of rain and

mist draped itself over the marsh, and I could hardly see — until the lightning lit the sky.

Faster, Sammy, faster, I told myself.

I tried to peer through the rain to see how far I had to go, but I couldn't even see the houses any more. That was bad enough.

But what I could see terrified me more.

Chapter Eleven

Something glimmered milky white through the sheets of rain. Now, it headed straight at me.

It was the ghost! Adam had told the truth after all!

The glimmer grew nearer, split in two, came closer, and closer still.

Then I heard it, like a whisper, just like Adam had said — only this time, it called *my* name.

"Samantha," it called. "Samantha."

Then, I swear, I heard a girl crying!

In a panic, I pedaled back the way I had come. The rain pounded in my ears.

And the ghost called me again, louder: "Samantha! Samantha!"

The glimmering lights were almost on top of me! My legs burned and I thought my heart would explode. The ghosts were faster than I was. I wasn't going to make it.

I heard the crying again.

"Sammmanthaaa!"

By now the lights were so close behind that they seemed to surround me. It was all over. I could not pedal any more.

"Samantha! Samantha McMillan!"

I knew that voice! It was Uncle Tim.

I hit the brakes. He was right behind me, in the car with Alfie, who was screaming at the top of his lungs.

"Uncle Tim!" I shouted. I'd never been so happy to see anyone in my life.

Lightning flashed across the sky.

"Put your bike by the side of the road and get in," he yelled out the window.

I jumped into the back seat. The glimmering must have been the headlights from the car. Funny, I could have sworn . . .

"Samantha McMillan," Uncle Tim scolded. "What the heck are you doing out on the marsh? Wasn't yesterday enough excitement for you? You're nothing but a lightning rod out here in a storm like this!"

"But what about my bike?" I asked meekly.

"You can get it later," he said. He'd gotten

soaked from leaning out the window. Alfie was wet too. That must have been why he was crying. But I could have sworn . . .

"The boys told me you disappeared on them this afternoon," Uncle Tim said.

"*Me*?" I said angrily. "*They* were the ones who disappeared!"

"Now, now," he said, "Don't get upset. I figured it was something like that."

By the time we pulled into the driveway, the rain had slowed to a drizzle.

"Listen," Uncle Tim said, as he unstrapped Alfie from his car seat, "this time of year, it rains almost every day. Usually late in the afternoon. I don't want to have to go looking for you again like that. If you see a storm coming, you stay away from the marsh. Got it?"

You bet I got it. I'd never been so scared in my life. What I didn't know then was that this was just the beginning.

Chapter Twelve

During dinner, the boys caught it for leaving me alone. They claimed they thought I was behind them.

Yeah, right.

When we finished eating, Uncle Tim sent them to their rooms. Under the circumstances, I decided not to ask anyone about the graveyard. Nobody was in a very good mood.

Later, after Aunt Sylvie put Alfie to bed, she called me into the living room. She was sitting on the sofa with a large photo album on her lap.

"Come sit," she said. "I want to show you something."

She pointed to the first picture. "This is me and your dad when he was about your age."

They were standing in the front yard of this very house. My dad was tall and skinny. He was squirting little Aunt Sylvie with a garden hose. I leaned over to look closely at him, but it was hard to see his face.

"Here, let me find a better one," Aunt Sylvie said.

She turned some pages, and I saw my dad again, dressed in a graduation cap and gown. He wore goofy glasses and he had long curly hair. His eyes were dark and almond-shaped. Like Aunt Sylvie's. Like Adam's.

Like mine.

I'd never seen pictures of my dad like this before. Mom only had a couple, and he looked a lot different.

Aunt Sylvie turned the pages.

"Here's Nana," she said, showing me a picture of an old lady on the beach.

"Who's Nana?" I asked.

Aunt Sylvie fell silent. She had a weird look on her face.

Finally, she said. "Has your mother told you about your dad and me growing up here? About our family?"

I shook my head.

Aunt Sylvie smiled. "Nana was my grand-mother," she said. "Your great-grandmother. She raised your dad and me. Here, in this house. This house has been in the McMillan family since the 1800s, when Nathaniel McMillan built it."

Nathaniel McMillan. I remembered his tombstone: *A loving father to us all.*

"And Nana?" I asked.

"She was his daughter," Aunt Sylvie said. "My mother died when I was born, so your dad and I came here to live with Nana."

"What about your father?"

"It would have been hard for him to take care of us. He was in the army. Lived on an army base, not far from here. He spent weekends with us, and holidays. But then he went to Vietnam. I'm sure there's a picture of him here somewhere."

She flipped through a few more pages.

"Here," she said. "This is how I remember him."

The picture showed a young man in green army pants and a T-shirt. He wore sun glasses, and he had short hair. He was quite handsome.

"That's my grandfather?" I asked, surprised.

"Sure is," Aunt Sylvie said.

"He doesn't look like a grandfather," I said.

Aunt Sylvie laughed. She pushed my bangs

away from my face, and stroked my hair.

"You know, Samantha," she said, "I see a lot of your dad in you. And he looked a lot like *his* dad. I think your dad would be really proud of you if he could see you today."

"I wish I'd known my dad," I said.

"Me too," Aunt Sylvie said.

"Can you tell me stories about him?" I asked. "Mom doesn't like to talk about him."

"Sure. But it's getting late," she said. "We'll talk more tomorrow."

She kissed me goodnight.

As I lay in bed trying to sleep, I kept thinking about all these new people in my family. People I hadn't known about before.

Usually I didn't miss my dad because I'd never really known him. But now I felt like I wanted to know everything. Finally I drifted off, thinking of my dad spraying *me* with a hose instead of Aunt Sylvie.

I'd only been asleep a few minutes when I heard someone calling my name.

"Samantha," the voice said, quiet and soft, like a lullaby. "Sammmannthaaaa . . . "

I opened my eyes. It sounded like Aunt Sylvie, but I wasn't sure. Why would Aunt Sylvie be calling me like that?

Then I heard it again, "Sammmmannthaaaa."

That was definitely *not* Aunt Sylvie. It came from outside. I sat up, leaned on the window sill, and scanned the back yard and Devil's Marsh beyond. The moon was bright.

Suddenly, a shadow raced across the grass and into the bushes. Then it darted out again. I held my breath.

I let out a deep sigh. It was just a cat chasing something. I must have been dreaming. I fell back into my pillow and closed my eyes.

Then I heard it again: "Sammmmannthaaaa . . . "

I clicked on the lamp and looked around the room. Everything looked normal.

"Sammmmannthaaaa McMilllllannnn . . . "

I got out of bed, lifted one of the hanging blankets, and peered out. The attic was dark. Shadows stretched along the floor.

I'd had enough scares for one day. I ran for the door, flew down the attic stairs, and raced down the hall toward Aunt Sylvie and Uncle Tim's bedroom.

But something stopped me in my tracks. I

stood alone, in the dark hallway, with my mouth gaping open.

I could not believe what I was seeing.

Chapter Thirteen

The door to Adam and Andy's room stood open. The boys had put a chair on top of Adam's bed, and Adam was standing on it, teetering, as Andy tried to hold it steady.

Adam looked up, saw me in the doorway, and lost his balance.

"Whoaaa!" he yelled, as he fell off the chair. He, Andy, and the chair crashed to the floor. Aunt Sylvie raced into the room in her nightie.

"What in the world?" she demanded angrily.

"Hi, Mom," Andy said, smiling his toothless grin.

Aunt Sylvie was not amused. "Get up this instant," she said. "What were you thinking, putting a chair on the bed? You could have broken your necks. Do you know what time it is?"

"Late?" Andy guessed.

"*Very* late," Aunt Sylvie snapped. "Not an-

other peep, do you hear me? Get to bed, Samantha."
She marched back down the hall and shut her door.

"Busted, dude," I sneered at Adam.

"What, busted? There's this big cobweb and
we were just trying to get this dead fly up there, to
feed the spider.

"He'th our pet," Andy said.

I looked at the ceiling. I didn't see any cob-
webs, but I did see a big vent right above Adam's bed.

"That must be a very talented spider," I said,
"Sort of like a parrot, huh? That you can teach to say
people's names?"

I turned on my heels and left. On my way back
upstairs, I heard Adam call, in that little sing-songy
voice of his, "Good night, Samantha."

I was so pooped my eyelids felt like lead
weights. I fell asleep at once.

But my dream — or should I say nightmare —
seemed as real as if I had been wide awake.

Chapter Fourteen

The full moon hangs low in the sky, casting a yellow glow over the graveyard. Shadows from the trees play on the tombstones. An owl hoots.

I sit on a stone bench outside the walls to the McMillan family plot. I am waiting for someone, but I don't know who.

Something cold and clammy slides over my bare feet. It's a black snake — like Rosie, only much bigger, with fiery yellow eyes. I am too terrified to move.

Slowly, she spirals up my leg. I hold my breath. She slithers under my shorts. I feel her spiky tongue flick my thigh. I can't stand it any longer.

"*AAAYYEEE!*" I scream. My hip burns as she bites, her teeth puncturing my skin again and again.

I jump up, trying to shake her off. Blood drips down my leg. Everything around me spins and I feel weak, as if I'm going to die. I fall to the ground.

But I don't die. Instead, my fall breaks the snake's hold on me, and it slithers away through the arched opening and into the family plot.

Behind the walls I hear two women arguing and scolding. They are angry.

One says, "Why did you have to treat her that way? She's just a child."

The other replies, "She has no right to be here. From the day she was born, she has broken my heart. And now she's done it again."

I try to get up, but the snake's poison has paralyzed my body. Eventually, I move my head enough so I can peek through the arch. I have to see who these women are.

Only, they aren't women.

It is the snake and the colorful little bird I had seen that afternoon.

The snake snaps her head in my direction.

"Hissssss," she says, and bares her fangs. The little bird, frightened, flies up into a tree.

The snake holds me in her stare, and I can't break away.

She opens her mouth. Poison drips down her fangs. With each drop, with each evil hiss, I feel her hatred of me just as surely as if she were biting me again and injecting her poison directly into my blood.

My heart burns. I want to look away, but I can't. My chest is on fire. Just when I think I can't take it anymore, the bird flies out of the tree and attacks the snake.

"Enough! Enough!" the bird cries.

The snake hisses at the bird, and tries to strike her. The bird flies away.

But now I am free from the snake's stare. Feeling returns to my body. I manage to get to my feet.

I run along the road and out to the marsh. The moon is so bright I have no trouble seeing. I cross the bridge and am about to pass the tree when something jumps at me.

The snake again! She's hanging from one of the branches.

"You hear what they cannot," she hisses. "You see what they cannot. This is how I will come to you. You have broken my heart and you must pay."

She tries to bite me, but this time I am too quick for her, and I race away.

Suddenly I hear a huge *CRACK!* Sparks shoot like fireworks from the center of the tree. The shape of a head forms, the ghostly head from Adam's story.

But this time it has the mouth of the snake, with razor-sharp fangs and a forked tongue.

I do not want to see if little things come flying out.

Running as fast as I can, I hear the ghost — the snake ghost — calling my name.

"Sammmmannthaaaa . . ."

I run all the way across the marsh.

"Sammmmannthaaaa . . ."

* * *

I sat up in bed, wide awake.

"Sammmmannthaaaa . . ."

That was no dream. It didn't sound like Adam, either. I looked around the room, and then out the window.

And what I saw was more real and more terrifying than any dream could ever be.

Chapter Fifteen

The moon was full, as it had been in my dream.

Deep in the marsh, I saw flashes of red and orange light. I smelled smoke.

Suddenly — *FLOOSH!* — flames shot into the sky. A fire blazed, right in the middle of the marsh!

I ran downstairs as fast as I could. As I raced past Adam and Andy's room, I saw the fire through their window, too. The flames rose as tall as a two-story building. Smoke billowed in a black cloud over the marsh. A chemical smell filled my nose.

I wondered how they could sleep through this. I ran down the hall to Aunt Sylvie and Uncle Tim's room and opened the door a crack.

"Aunt Sylvie," I whispered, "I'm sorry to wake you, but . . ."

"What is it, Samantha?" she asked.

As I stepped into the room, I noticed their window looked out on the marsh, too, and . . . and . . .

I saw nothing. No fire. No smoke. No smell. The marsh looked quiet and peaceful.

"I'm sorry," I stammered. "I thought I saw something outside, but I guess I was dreaming."

"All right then," Aunt Sylvie said, and rolled over. As I walked past Adam and Andy's room, I looked out their window again. Nothing.

Boy, that was weird.

Back in my room, I was scared to go back to sleep. I looked out the window at the marsh for a long time. A gentle breeze blew, and everything was quiet. I decided the whole thing must have been a dream.

Perhaps my conscience had been bothering me. I felt guilty about breaking the angel and taking the little heart. I decided to tell Aunt Sylvie about it in the morning.

I tried to go back to sleep, but every time I closed my eyes the image of the fire came back to me. Even the smell.

I sat up and rummaged through my stuff for one of my books. Maybe reading will help, I thought.

The next thing I knew, I woke up to the sun shining through the window. My book lay open across my chest, and I had a horrible headache.

"Samantha, your mom's on the phone," Aunt

Sylvie called from downstairs.

I grabbed my robe and rushed to the phone. It made me happy to hear Mom's voice. I wanted to tell her about getting lost. About the graveyard, and my bad dream. About how awful the boys were.

But when she asked how I was, I just said fine. I didn't want to upset her.

"Aunt Sylvie showed me some cool pictures of Dad when he was a kid," I said.

Mom was quiet for a moment, and then she said, "Really?"

"Yeah, and Nana, too."

"Nana?" My mother sounded surprised. "What did she tell you about Nana?"

"Just about how Nana took care of Dad and her."

"I see." Mom sounded sort of weird.

"Is something wrong?" I asked.

"Oh, no," Mom answered quickly. "I think it's good for you to learn about your dad's family."

She said she'd call again soon, and that she loved me.

Aunt Sylvie wanted to talk, so I gave her the phone. My head was pounding. I wandered out to the front porch. Adam and Andy were playing marbles in the driveway.

"Hey, Thammy," Andy called. The boys wore cut-offs, no shirts, and baseball caps turned backwards on their heads. Adam actually smiled at me.

Well, maybe this would be a better day. I sat down with them.

"Your mom call?" Adam asked as he took a shot.

"Uh-huh."

"How's France?"

"OK, I guess."

"I thee London. I thee Franth. I thee Thammy's underpanth," Andy sang.

"You know what?" I said. "You guys slept through the strangest thing last night."

"Yeah? What?" Adam said, as he lined up his next shot. I noticed he stuck his tongue out when he concentrated.

He flicked the marble right on target. *Bink!* It knocked two of the last three marbles outside the circle.

"Yes!" Adam gloated. He threw his arms over his head and laughed. Offended, Andy ran into the house.

"Why do you have to be so mean?" I asked.

"I'm not mean," Adam said. "So, what did I miss last night? Any ghoulie little ghosties try to crawl in your ear?"

"No," I said. I wondered now if I should even tell him or not.

"What then?" Adam asked.

"Well," I said, because I was dying to tell somebody, "I had this really bad dream, and it woke me up, so then I was awake."

"Oh, that's *so* interesting, Samantha," Adam said.

I realized I sounded stupid. Something about Adam always made me feel tongue-tied.

"OK," I said, "so then I looked out the window, and I saw . . . "

"The ghost!" Adam teased.

"No. Listen. I saw a fire. In the middle of the marsh. It was huge. Flames. Smoke. Everything. I ran downstairs to get your folks, but by the time I got to their room it was gone. You guys slept through the whole thing."

"Wait a minute . . . " Adam said, suddenly serious. "You saw a fire in Devil's Marsh?"

"Yeah. It just shot up from nowhere. And then, poof, it went out."

Adam studied me. "It's just that . . . "

"What?" I asked.

"That's one of the other stories about Devil's Marsh. One of the ghost stories I didn't tell you the other night."

We looked at each other, stunned.

"Tell me now," I said, even though I was afraid of what I might hear.

"You know how the road is really narrow through the marsh?"

I nodded.

"Well, there have been lots of car wrecks out there. Sometimes when it gets real foggy, it's hard to see.

"OK. So, there's this old lady whose husband died a long time ago, and now she lives with her son. He is all she has. And she's really weird. Doesn't let him do stuff, even though he's a grownup and all.

"Anyway, one day he meets this girl and falls in love. The old lady freaks. She can't handle the idea of him leaving her. She forbids him to see her.

"One night they are driving through the marsh and the son tells the mother he's going to get married. They start fighting. The old lady goes nuts. Just then, she sees the headlights from another car, and she yells,

'I'll kill you before I let you leave me!' She grabs the steering wheel and they slam head-on into the other car. Both cars catch fire and, *WOOSH*, everybody goes up in flames.

"Now, sometimes, at night, people see a fire shoot up in the middle of the marsh. And then it will just disappear.

"There's this kid I know, Marty Thomas. He swears his dad saw the fire driving home one night. He thought it was an accident and he went to check it out. When he got to the spot, there was nothing.

"He got out of his car to look around. That's when he heard a baby crying and lots of screaming. And there was this weird smell, like rubber burning.

"He figured the cars had hit so hard they'd shot off into the marsh. So he drove to a house at the edge of the marsh to call the police. But nobody ever found anything."

I shuddered. "My dad died in a car accident," I said.

"I'm sorry," Adam said.

"That's OK," I said. "It was a long time ago."

We were both quiet for a minute.

"So, you think I saw the fire?" I asked. "That it was a ghost thing?"

"What else could it be?"

"Adam, I need to tell you something else," I said. I knew I was taking a risk. I didn't know if I could trust him. Maybe he would use what I said to set me up for some huge joke.

It didn't matter. I had to tell someone about all the weird stuff that was going on.

<u>Chapter Sixteen</u>

I took a deep breath.

"A lot of weird stuff happened yesterday," I said. "First I met this witch . . ."

"What do you mean, witch?" Adam interrupted.

"She lives on the edge of town in that little shack. Live Crabs, Casts Spells."

Adam laughed. "Oh, you mean Nadina. She's no witch. She's just a crazy old lady."

"She seemed pretty creepy to me," I said. "She waved her hands all over me and said scary stuff."

"She does that to everybody. Big deal!"

I hated the way Adam made me feel stupid. I didn't feel like telling him about anything else now, not the graveyard, or the dream or anything. I got up, brushed off my pants, and walked back to the house.

"You are such a *girl*!" Adam yelled after me.

Exactly, I thought. And you are such a *boy*.

Inside, I found Aunt Sylvie leaving for work. "You stick close to home today," she said on her way out the door.

I heard the TV in the den. The Flintstones! My headache was going away and I realized I was hungry, so I got a bowl of cereal and joined Andy in the den.

"Hey," he said when I sat down next to him. He was still pouting over the marbles. We'll just sit here and watch TV and both be mad at Adam, I thought.

But Adam joined us.

"Go away," Andy muttered.

Adam ignored him. "Samantha," he said.

"Her name is *Thammy*," Andy snarled.

Adam rolled his eyes. "Sammy," he said. "Tell me exactly what Nadina said."

"You talked to Nadina?" Andy exclaimed, his eyes wide.

"Please tell me what she said," Adam repeated.

This was going to be sweet.

"Beg me," I said. "Get down on your hands and knees and beg me."

"Aw, come on," he said.

"Down," I said, pointing.

And he did it! He actually got down on the

floor, looked up at me and said, "Sammy, please, please tell me what Nadina said."

Man, he was serious! How could I not tell him?

"She said 'You've got the devil's power. I see it all around you,' or something like that."

"Are you sure that's what she said?" Adam asked.

"Yeah. Why?" He was starting to make me nervous.

"This sounds crazy," Adam said, "but after you told me about the fire, and now, with what Nadina said about devil's power . . . Well, you know what she was talking about, don't you?"

"No. What?" I said.

"When did you thee Nadina? What fire?" Andy said, tugging at my shirt.

"Remember my story about the lightning?" Adam said.

"How could I forget?"

"What are you guyth talking about?" Poor Andy was about to pop.

"We'll explain in a minute," Adam said to him. Then he looked back at me. "What I told you was true," he said. "I mean, it's a real story."

"Yeah, right," I said.

"OK, maybe it didn't happen to me, exactly, but it's true that people around here believe that if you get hit by lightning, it gives you the power to see ghosts and stuff."

"But I didn't get hit by lightning," I said.

"Yeah, but maybe it was close enough," Adam said. "Sammy, don't you get it?"

"Get what?" Andy and I said at the same time.

"Look. First, you nearly get hit by lightning. Then you bump into Nadina who says she sees the devil's power around you, and then last night you see this mystery fire. How could Nadina have known you'd been zapped — unless she really could see something?"

"Like an aura?" I asked.

"What'th an aura?" Andy asked.

"It's like light or something, coming from your body. Some people say they can see it," Adam said.

"Cool," Andy said.

But I didn't think it was so cool. I sat quietly. I had to think.

Chapter Seventeen

"What else happened yesterday?" Adam asked.

"I went to the graveyard," I said quietly. Talking about it made me afraid now.

"Thee, Adam!" Andy shouted. "I told you Thammy'd go ghotht hunting!"

"I wasn't ghost hunting," I said. "I was lost — *remember* — and I just stumbled on it. I saw a beautiful bird, and he seemed to be calling me, and I walked around and saw the McMillan plot."

"Oh, man," Adam said. "You didn't go inside, did you?"

"Of course I went inside."

Andy jumped up and down on the couch. "Oh, Thammy, you are tho brave!" he shouted. "Even Adam won't go inthide."

"It's cursed," Adam said. "Nadina said it was full of evil spirits and no McMillan should ever step inside the walls."

"You told me no one pays attention to Nadina," I said.

"Yeah, but why take chances?"

"Did you thee anything?" Andy asked me.

I lowered my eyes. I had to tell someone. "I knocked an angel off one of the tombstones and it broke," I confessed.

"Oh, no," Adam moaned, shaking his head. "The worst thing you can do is upset a grave!"

"How was I supposed to know!" I shot back. "It was an accident!"

"Oooooo, Thammy," Andy shook his head too, imitating Adam.

"Cut it out!" I shouted. "It was an accident! Besides, if *you two* hadn't left me alone, I wouldn't have gotten lost in the first place!"

I stormed out of the den and up to my room. I felt like crying. Then, I remembered what the snake ghost had said in my dream. I had broken her heart, and I had to pay.

How had I gotten into this mess?

Adam pulled one of the blankets aside and poked his head into my room.

"Look, maybe it's all just superstition," he said. "Just forget about it."

"I can't," I said. "It's already started."

Now I really was crying. Adam sat down on the bed next to me.

"Maybe you didn't really see the fire," he said. "Maybe it was just a reflection in the window, or maybe . . ."

"No," I said. "It's not just the fire."

And so I told Adam about my dream. I was so upset that I didn't see Andy come into my room, too.

"Thammy, are you OK?" he asked.

"What am I going to do?" I wailed.

We all sat quietly and tried to think. Finally Adam looked up. "There's no other way," he said. "We have to go see Nadina, to get her to take the curse off."

"Are you crazy! I'm not going back there!"

"What else can you do?" Adam said.

"I can go home," I cried.

"Ghosts don't care about where you live, Sammy. They'll just follow you."

"Thammy," Andy said, puffing himself up. "We'll go with you. Huh, Adam?"

"Sure we will," Adam said, putting his hand on my shoulder. Maybe he wasn't so bad after all. "We'll go get your bike, and then ride to Nadina's house."

The morning was sweet and clear. Puffy clouds floated above us. The smell of salt water hung in the air. We heard the sea gulls calling and the neighbor's patio chimes tinkling in the breeze. The sun warmed my back as we walked.

Maybe, I thought, when we finished this Nadina business, we could play on the beach. Adam walked his bike beside me while Andy rode circles around us.

One block more, another corner, and we stood in front of Devil's Marsh. It opened flat and wide, reminding me of the ocean. It was hard to imagine this place had been so terrifying the night before. The marsh grass shifted in the breeze. The insects hummed.

"Samantha?"

I turned my head around. "What?"

Adam looked up. He'd been watching his feet. "What?" he asked.

"What, what?" I said. "Didn't you just say something?"

Adam shook his head.

I stopped walking. "Please tell me you just called my name," I said.

He shook his head again. "I swear," he said.

We stood quietly for a moment. I listened hard. All I heard was the grass whispering in the breeze.

"Come on," Adam said, "you're just spooking yourself."

Andy was way ahead of us. He rounded a bend and disappeared from sight. Adam called to him to slow down, but he didn't hear us. Adam got on his bike.

"Hurry," he said to me. "Andy's almost at the bridge and I don't want him on it by himself. It's too narrow. If a car comes, he'll freak."

Adam whizzed off. I tried to run to keep up, but I'm not a good runner. I stopped and bent over to catch my breath.

That's when I heard it again.

"Samantha, how dare you?" the voice hissed. It sounded like a woman's voice, like the voice I'd heard in my dream!

I looked around. I saw no one, and now Adam was out of sight, too.

I started running again, but the voice stayed with me.

"You will pay," it whispered. "You will payyyyy!"

I cupped my hands over my ears, but it didn't help. The voice was inside my head and it wouldn't stop.

"You'll never be be able to run away," the voice said, and cackled wickedly.

"Stop it!" I screamed. "Stop it!"

Then I heard something so horrible it drowned out even the laughing in my head.

Chapter Eighteen

The bone-chilling cry came from around the bend. Andy was screaming hysterically.

"No!" I shouted, running as fast as I could. "Please, not Andy! Whatever you are, please leave him alone!"

I cleared the bend and almost slammed into Adam, who stared in horror at the bridge in front of us.

Andy was halfway across the bridge, pressed against the railing, screaming. At the other end of the bridge, in the middle of the road, sat an alligator! It must have crawled out of the marsh!

"Don't move," Adam said to me. "Andy, quiet!" he called, as sternly as he could without being too loud. Andy clamped his jaw shut, but he was shaking all over.

The alligator must have been eight feet long. It squatted in the middle of the road, its spiky tail flipping back and forth. It opened its mouth and hissed like a snake. I screamed and jumped back.

"Shhh," Adam snapped.

"Chhhhhhhaaaaaaaaa," the alligator hissed again.

"Adam, do something!" Andy cried.

Adam grabbed some rocks from the edge of the road, keeping his eyes on Andy and the alligator.

The alligator swished its tail and walked a few steps closer to Andy.

"Adam!" Andy yelled.

"Back up," Adam called. "Real slow."

"He's going to get me!" Andy cried, too terrified to move.

The laughing started in my head again. "You will pay! You will *all* pay!"

"*NOOO!*" I screamed.

The alligator charged, his yellow eyes blazing. His thick, green body darted across the bridge. Right for Andy.

Adam hurled a rock, smacking the alligator on the nose. It swung its head around to see what had hit it. Adam lobbed more rocks, pelting the alligator.

"Go, Andy, GO!" he yelled.

The alligator hissed furiously and snapped his

jaws. He lurched across the bridge after Andy, who ran as fast as he could. But he was no match for the alligator.

The alligator got closer and closer. I screamed!

"Now!" the evil voice in my head hissed like the alligator. "Noowwwww!"

Suddenly, a car barreled down the road from the other side of the bridge, traveling much too fast.

Andy made it to the end of bridge and jumped to the side of the road. The driver slammed on the brakes. The car barely missed the alligator, which skittered off the edge of the bridge and slipped into the water.

The car stopped and one of Allen's friends got out. He reached for Andy, who was shaking like a leaf.

"Hey, Andy, it's OK now," he said. "You want me to put your bike in the trunk and take you home?"

Andy nodded. He couldn't even talk.

"How about you guys?" the boy asked. "Want a lift?"

"No. But thanks," I said.

The voice in my head was quiet, but I knew now that something horrible and evil had taken root inside me.

And I knew the alligator had not arrived by coincidence.

Adam was right. I had to go see Nadina. Now.

Chapter Nineteen

I waited to see whether Adam would go home or stay with me.

"Yeah, we've got stuff to do," he said. "Thanks, though." He wasn't going to let me down.

We watched the car round the bend and disappear behind the tall grass.

"Where's your bike?" Adam asked as we crossed the bridge.

"Near the tree," I said. I looked up and met Adam's gaze. "The voice came back," I said. "Like it was in my dream. It's the snake ghost, Adam. I know it is."

"Do you hear it now?" he asked.

"No."

"Then let's keep going. Nadina will help us."

Down the road, I could see the tree — one half dead, one half full of life.

My bike lay in the grass beside the road. I

grabbed the seat and tried to pull it from the grass, but the front tire was caught. I yanked hard, and the bike popped loose.

But when I looked at it, I almost fainted.

"*AAAAIIIIEEEE!*" I screamed.

"What is it?" Adam said, rushing over.

Hundreds of black, slimy eels, slithered over each other in my bicycle basket.

"Drop the bike!" Adam yelled.

I threw it to the ground. The impact knocked the eels from the basket, and they squirmed away toward the water.

The laughing started in my head, and grew louder and louder. I held my head in my hands. It hurt to open my eyes.

"Adam," I cried, "it's happening again!"

"Sammy, Sammy" Adam called. I could barely hear him.

"Listen to me," he shouted, pulling my hands from my ears. "Tell it to stop. *Think* it away. Fight it!"

"I can't!" I cried.

"You have to," he said. "Try!"

"Go away!" I screamed. "I've done nothing to hurt you! Leave me alone!"

"Nothing, you say!" the voice screamed back

at me. "First you broke my heart and then you stole it!"

"It was an accident! I didn't mean to!"

"You will pay," she said. "You will pay." But her voice grew softer and softer. Finally it faded away.

I opened my eyes and looked at Adam. "Is it over?" he asked.

I nodded. I picked up my bike. The grips on the handle bars were sticky and gross.

Adam wiped them off with the bottom of his shirt.

"Adam," I asked, "do you think I'm crazy?"

"Nope," he said.

"Are you scared?"

"Yep," he said. At least he was honest.

"Me too," I said. And then I added, "I'm glad you're here, though."

"I'm not," he said, smiling weakly. "Let's go."

We continued through the marsh. As we passed the burnt tree, I looked away to avoid seeing anything evil hanging from a branch. But nothing happened. We made our way along the edge of the marsh. I jumped at every little sound. We kept riding.

As we were about to clear the tall grass, the voice came back.

"It's not over yet," she whispered.

Chapter Twenty

"Adam, stop!" I called out.

"What is it?"

But the voice had fallen silent again.

"Listen," I said. "Do we have to go past the graveyard?"

"Yeah. Unless you want to go back through the marsh and around through town."

"No, no. Forget it," I said. But I thought we were nuts to go near the graveyard.

We rode past the live oaks and palms until we were deep in the woods. The closer to the graveyard we got, the more frightened I became.

There it was, on the right. Maybe if I just didn't look at it . . . I turned toward the left side of the road.

"*AAAEEEHHH!*"

The snake ghost swung from the trees above my head. It was huge, white and vapory. I could see right through it. Its eyes burned like hot coals, just like in my dream. I saw the dripping fangs and the flickering tongue.

"Now, Samantha," it hissed, "the revenge is mine."

My bike flew out of control and shot into the road. A truck roared around the corner heading right at me!

"*SAMMY!*" Adam yelled.

The truck veered into the other lane. The driver honked angrily as the big rig sped by.

"Sammy, are you OK?" Adam panted.

"Adam, it was so horrible," I whimpered, shaking. "The snake ghost was hanging from the tree. Didn't you see it?"

"Samantha," Adam said. "I don't see anything. I don't hear anything. I'm sorry."

"Oh, Adam," I sobbed. "I don't know how much more I can take."

"Come on," Adam said. "We're almost there. You can do it."

I had no choice. We mounted our bikes.

"What's the happiest song you know?" Adam asked as we rode.

"Happiest? I don't know. John Jacob Jingleheimer Smith."

"Come on, Samantha," he said. "Let's sing that ghost out of your head."

We sang about a zillion verses of John Jacob Jingleheimer Smith, all the way to Nadina's little shack. At the top of our lungs. And it worked. The ghost left us alone for the rest of the way.

If it had been that easy to get rid of the curse, I would have sung John Jacob Jingleheimer Smith for the rest of the summer.

But it wasn't that easy. Not at all.

Chapter Twenty-One

Considering how badly Nadina had scared me the day before, I was awfully glad to see her shack appear through the trees.

"She's usually over there," Adam said, pointing to a couple of old lawn chairs under a tree. Aluminum pie plates hung from the tree, and bits of foil caught the sunlight. Empty crab traps were piled by the door. A spicy smell filled the yard.

"Crab boil," Adam said. "You use it when you cook crab."

He knocked on the door.

Someone fumbled with the lock, and the door creaked open. It was Nadina, all right. I could tell by the bony fingers wrapped around the edge of the door, wearing orange nail polish. And I smelled that nasty smell, like spoiled egg salad.

"What do you want?" she snapped.

"It's me, Miss Nadina," Adam said. "Adam

Dimswell."

"Got no more crab today," Nadina said, shutting the door.

"Wait. It's not about crab."

The door opened again. Nadina, only as tall as we were, stood in the doorway. Her hazy eyes bulged like a bullfrog's. A turban enclosed her hair, but gray curls poked out.

"What do you want that's not crab," she asked suspiciously.

Adam pushed me in front of him, so Nadina could see me. She jumped back as if I were diseased.

"Oh, no, no, no," She clucked. "She got the devil power. No, no, no."

"Miss Nadina, please," Adam begged. "This is my cousin. Samantha McMillan."

Nadina stuck a pointy finger in Adam's face.

"You don't have to tell me that, boy. I sees it with my own blind eyes. I sees the power, and I sees the McMillan, too. I knowed her the second I laid these blind eyes on her. She done come back. And Miz Sam don' like it none." Nadina let out a mean little chuckle.

"What is she talking about?" I asked.

"Miss Nadina, could we please talk to you?"

Adam begged. "We need your help."

"Yes sir, I bet you do," Nadina laughed. "All right then, but not in the house. No negative energy allowed in my house."

She pushed past us, hobbled to the lawn chairs and sat in one. I took the other. Adam sat on the grass. Nadina lit a stick of cinnamon incense and waved it over our heads.

She held out her hand. "Twenty dollars," she said.

I looked at Adam, surprised. I didn't know that we were expected to pay money. But he didn't flinch.

"I'll bring it tomorrow," he said.

She cocked her head to the side, and pursed her lips in and out. "You do not cheat Nadina, little man?" she said.

"Never," Adam said.

She leaned back, crossed her arms, and sighed deeply. She closed her eyes and muttered words I could not understand. When she opened her eyes, she looked different somehow, more clear-headed.

She looked me straight in the eye for a long time. It made me feel weird, as if she were looking deep inside me, seeing everything.

"You in deep trouble, girl," She said. "You got the devil in you, for sure. Miz Sam's devil."

"You mean, my devil?" I asked shyly.

"Not you," Nadine scolded. "Miz Sam! You made her very, very mad."

I turned to Adam, "Miz Sam?"

"Nana," he said.

"Nana!" I exclaimed. Miz Sam was Nana? And she was mad at me?

Nadina leaned forward and grabbed my chin with her long, bony fingers. "Listen, child, you got to make your peace or she will destroy you. You understand *that*?"

"Yes, but . . . "

"She already got you, girl. She in you like a boll weevil and she will eat your brain from the insides out. Do you understand *that*? You got the lightnin' power to see, to hear. Then you go and upset the dead. Not smart, girl. Specially when the dead be mad already. So mad, her evil energies take over and make her take on evil forms. Now, you do what Nadina says.

"You get a picture of Miz Sam. After midnight, you take it to the grave, and . . ." She stopped short and squinted at me.

"Did you take something that belong to her?"

I nodded, ashamed. Adam looked at me, surprised.

"You take it back. You tell her you sorry. Then you take that picture and you burn it. Bury the ashes by the headstone. Then empty your heart, and fill it with love. It be the only way, child."

"Empty my heart? What do you mean?"

"Cast out all your fears, all your sadness and anger. All your negative energies. And fill it back up with love. With compassion. Miz Sam, she been in pain for so long. To free yourself, child, you have to free her, too."

I looked at Adam, terrified. Nadina was no help. Cast out my fears? How the heck was I supposed to do that?

Nadina fished in the pocket of her caftan and pulled out a small blue candle. "Use this to burn the picture. It's blessed. Will help you clear the evil power."

"Thank you, Miss Nadina," Adam said. He got up to go.

But I wasn't ready to leave.

"Miss Nadina, why is Miss Sam so mad at me? Is it just the broken angel? That was an accident. I know I shouldn't have taken the heart, but it was cracked, so I didn't think it mattered to anyone."

Nadina looked at me with pity in her milky eyes.

"Girl, you go ask your auntie about that. That's not for Nadina to tell. I clear the secrets for the dead, child, not the living,"

"What do you think she meant by that?" I asked Adam as we rode back.

"Beats me," said Adam.

We went through town, to avoid the marsh. We stopped at Dennis's Super-Duper Ice Cream Extravaganza and got Denny to give us some free sodas. Then we walked out to the pier and sat down to think.

"Adam?" I asked. "Do you believe all that stuff she said will work?"

"I don't know," Adam said. "But what else can we do?"

"Maybe we should talk to your folks about this," I suggested.

"Yeah, right." Adam imitated my voice, making it sound high and prissy. "Excuse me, Aunt Sylvie, but I think I'm possessed by the ghost of my great-grandmother, who comes to me like a snake and screams in my head, and makes my bike fly into trucks."

"Don't forget alligators and eels," I said.

"And fire," Adam said, slurping the last of his soda.

"I don't think I can go back to that graveyard in the middle of the night."

"Do you want to be rid of this ghost thing or not?" Adam asked.

Out in the ocean, the fishing boats bobbed on the water. I saw children making sand castles on the beach. I watched seagulls dive into the waves. Sitting there, it was easy to feel like the whole thing had just been a bad dream. Just my imagination running wild.

But I knew that wasn't true. And I knew I wasn't crazy.

Maybe no one else could see the ghost or hear it, but it was real to me. And there was no telling when it would start haunting me again. Adam was right.

We had to go back to the graveyard that night.

Chapter Twenty-Two

Andy was crazy with curiosity when we got back to the house.

"What'd she thay?" he demanded. Adam and I had already decided not to tell him anything, because then he'd want to go to the graveyard with us.

"She waved her hand over Sammy's head, like this," Adam said, "and muttered, 'Ippsy pippsy wiggum woo, make the power fly from you.' "

Andy's eyes nearly popped out of his head. I turned away so he wouldn't see me laughing.

Adam put his arm around his brother and escorted him to the den. It was part of our plan. Now, I was supposed to get the photo album and sneak out Nana's picture.

I tiptoed into the living room. The album was on the coffee table. I stuffed it under my shirt and ran upstairs to my room.

I removed the picture of Nana that Aunt Sylvie

had shown me from the album and looked at it closely. Nana's face was hidden behind sunglasses and a hat. I turned the picture over. On the back someone had written, *Summer 1987*.

I remembered the date on the tombstone. That was the summer Nana died. Creepy.

"What is it, Nana?" I asked. "What did I do that made you so mad?"

A gust of wind blew through my window like a hurricane. It tore the blankets from the ropes and ripped the album from my lap, scattering pictures everywhere and knocking me off the bed. I bumped my head on the edge of the desk.

But now, instead of feeling scared, I was mad. Really mad.

I crawled across the floor, grabbed my shorts, and pulled the cracked heart from my pocket. I squeezed it as tightly as I could.

"Stop it now!" I shouted to the wind. "Or I'll crush your heart to bits. I swear it!"

"You couldn't even if you wanted to," the voice laughed in my head.

"Just watch me!" I shouted back. I reached for one of Andy's metal cars and lifted it to smash the little heart.

The wind stopped.

The attic door flew open. Andy and Adam rushed in.

"What happened?" Adam asked. But he knew it was the ghost.

"Thammy?" Andy asked, with big, frightened eyes. Adam shook his head. He didn't want Andy to know.

"Yeah, um, Andy," I said, smiling. "You're not going to believe this but, um, I was doing this spinning dance that I like to do, and I, um, get kind of crazy and I throw things. It feels really good, but it makes a big mess sometimes."

"Sure does," Andy said. It was a stupid lie, but he seemed to believe it. He went back downstairs.

Adam flopped onto the sofa. "Man, look at this place," he said. "What happened?"

"Wind. Lots of it."

"I guess so," he said. "Did you get the Nana picture?"

"Yeah, but look," I said. The rest of the pictures were strewn all over the floor. "We'll never be able to put them back in order."

"No big deal," Adam said. "We'll hide it in Alfie's room and tell Mom he did it. He does stuff like that all the time. And he won't get in trouble 'cause he's a baby."

Adam and I spent the rest of the afternoon discussing our plans for sneaking out.

All through dinner I was nervous and jittery. Afterwards, Uncle Tim and the boys piled into the den to watch a baseball game. But I couldn't pay attention.

I kept thinking about the snake ghost. And that stuff Nadina had said about the secrets of the living. What was I supposed to ask Aunt Sylvie, anyway?

Suddenly, I heard it: "Samantha."

I froze. It was the voice. She was back!

Chapter Twenty-Three

"Samantha," the voice said. "Have you seen the photo album? I wanted to show you some more pictures."

I breathed a deep sigh and shook my head. It was just Aunt Sylvie.

"That's strange," she said, "I was sure I left it on the coffee table."

I followed her to the living room and pretended to help her look.

"Aunt Sylvie, tell me more about Nana," I said.

"Nana?" Aunt Sylvie asked. "Samantha, it's hard to talk about Nana because I don't want to give you the wrong impression. Nana wasn't a mean or bad person. She was just very unhappy. Sometimes her unhappiness made her difficult to get along with."

You're telling me, I thought.

"I know your mom hasn't said much about Nana or the McMillans, but it's for a good reason. When your mom and I talked this morning, we decided it was time you knew. But I haven't discussed this with the boys because it simply hasn't come up. So this is just between you and me. OK?"

I nodded.

"Let's go for a little walk," Aunt Sylvie suggested.

We crossed the street and cut through the dunes to the beach. It was low tide and the sand stretched for miles. The moon cast a silvery light on the ocean. We walked along the edge of the water, getting our feet wet.

"You see," Aunt Sylvie said, "Nana always felt that everyone she cared about deserted her. It wasn't true, but that's how she felt. Her husband — my grandfather — left her for another woman. It was a horrible scandal. That's when she moved back to the house, to live with her father, Nathaniel McMillan. But he was very old and died soon after. There was very little money, and it was rough for Nana.

"Did she ever remarry?" I asked.

"No, she never did. She poured all her energies into her son. That was my dad. When he was killed in

Vietnam, she went to pieces.

"She was never quite right after that. It's hard to explain, Samantha. She just wasn't a very strong person. She blamed other people for her own unhappiness.

"I was pretty young when I married your Uncle Tim," Aunt Sylvie said. "Nana was furious. She refused to come to the wedding."

"Didn't that make you feel bad?" I asked.

"Oh sure," she said, "but I got over it. I couldn't live with her forever."

"What about my dad?"

"Your dad lived with Nana for a long, long time. He talked about leaving, but Nana always made him feel guilty, and he'd stay. Then he met your mother."

"How?" I asked.

"On the beach, right around here, actually. She was on vacation and she rented a sailboat from your dad. It was love at first sight. They spent every day together for two weeks. And when your mom's vacation was over, and they realized they'd have to be apart, they decided to get married."

"After two weeks!"

"Samantha, it didn't matter. It was as if they

had known each other their whole lives. Well, as you can imagine, poor Nana flipped. Your dad was all she had left.

"So your dad and your mom eloped. Just ran off and got married. Nana decided she'd have nothing to do with them after that. She wouldn't talk to them. She'd send their letters back unopened.

"When you were born, they named you after her, thinking that would help. But it only made her angrier. She felt they were mocking her."

"I don't get it," I said.

"I don't either," Aunt Sylvie sighed. "Anyway, right around your first birthday, Nana got very sick. She was old, and we didn't think she would live much longer. Your dad wanted to make peace with her before she died. So he brought you and your mom back to Bart's Island. He thought maybe if Nana could see you and hold you, she would see how happy you all were, and she'd forgive him."

"Did she?" I asked.

Aunt Sylvie looked out at the water. Her eyes got misty.

"No, she didn't. They started arguing, and she got so upset she had a heart attack. Or at least that's what she said. Nana tended to overreact. It was late at night, and we were having one of our famous storms. So your dad piled you and your mom and Nana into the car to take her to the hospital. As they were going through the marsh . . . "

Aunt Sylvie wiped a tear from her cheek.

"As they were going through the marsh, a car coming the other way slid in the rain and hit your dad's car. Both cars went up in flames. Your mom was thrown from the car, but your dad and you and Nana were locked inside. Your dad managed to get out and he grabbed you, but the car exploded before he could get to Nana. He tried and tried, yanking on the door of the flaming car. His burns were so bad that he died a few days later."

I didn't know what to say. I knew my dad had died in a car accident, but Mom had never told me any of this.

Now everything made sense. Now I understood why Nana's ghost was so angry with me. She saw me and my mom as the people who took my dad away from her. And when the car burned, he saved me first.

Now I knew what Nadina meant about me having to free Nana's spirit.

I wanted to tell Aunt Sylvie about Nana's

ghost and our plans to go to the graveyard. But I knew that, if I did, she wouldn't let us go. And then what?

"It's not a pretty story is it?" Aunt Sylvie said. "The thing to remember is that your dad loved you and your mom very much. And Nana too. Even if she didn't believe it.

"You know," she added, "there's even a ghost story about the crash that night. Some people say they've seen the fire in the marsh, late at night. They've heard screams, and a baby crying. I guess that baby would be you."

I shivered. This was too weird.

"But there's no such thing as ghosts. This island is full of superstitions about things that have logical explanations. People like to let their imaginations run wild, I guess."

"Yeah, I guess," I said, wishing Aunt Sylvie was right. But I knew she was wrong.

Chapter Twenty-Four

"Psst. Sammy, you ready?" It was Adam, calling up the stairs.

Ready? I'd gone to bed with my clothes on. I'd tossed back and forth for hours.

"Got the picture and the heart?"

"What do you think?" I snapped. I felt cranky and tired. And I was scared silly. "What about the candle?" I asked.

"Check."

"Matches? Glue?"

"Double check."

We crept down the stairs and slipped out the door. In seconds we were on our bikes.

"That was too easy," I said. I'd never been out late at night before. It was so quiet I could hear the waves pounding the beach behind the dunes. The moon was still bright, so it was easy to see. The lights were off in most of the houses.

It felt like the whole island was asleep but us.

We decided to ride through town instead of through Devil's Marsh. No way was I going in there at night.

Soon we were on Main Street. All the shops were closed. Cars were parked down by the pier, and we could see people fishing in the dark. A police car turned the corner. The lights almost blinded us.

"Come on," Adam said. I followed him into an alley where we waited until the police passed.

"Let's take the side streets. It will be easier," he said. We cut through the alley, made some quick turns, and headed toward the graveyard.

The trees blocked the moon, and I had more trouble seeing. Adam had a light on his bike, but I didn't. A dog shot out from nowhere, barking and snapping.

"Pump it!" Adam yelled.

I pedaled as hard as I could. I felt the dog's breath as he tried to bite my heels.

"Faster, Sammy, faster!" Adam yelled.

I went as fast as I could make my legs go. But the dog wouldn't quit. Just when I thought he'd given up, he'd gain speed again and snap at my heels.

Then the strangest thing happened. The dog

suddenly stopped. He took off in the other direction, whimpering. Something had scared him.

Adam had stopped and was straddling his bike. I looked up. We were in front of the gate to the graveyard.

<u>Chapter Twenty-Five</u>

Everything seemed quiet. I hadn't heard from the ghost since the windstorm in my bedroom. Maybe this wasn't going to be that bad after all.

"You ready?" Adam asked. I saw his hands shake as he leaned his bike against the fence.

"Hey Adam," I said. "Thanks for coming with me tonight."

Adam pretended he didn't hear me. "Let's get this over with," he said. He flipped the flashlight on and we walked inside.

I'd barely gone two steps when I felt something move under my shoe.

I jumped. A black snake slithered in and out of the flashlight beam as it rushed for the bushes.

"Adam," I said, "that's the snake in my dream."

"We've got snakes like that all over the place," Adam said. "They're like Rosie. They can't hurt you."

He moved his flashlight around the graveyard. It was a lot creepier than it had been during the day.

"Whoo! Whooo!" Adam shone his flashlight into a tree just in time to see an owl. Frightened by the light, it flew off.

"I wonder where my little bird friend is," I said to myself.

Adam shone the light on the McMillan wall. "Let's go," he said.

We made our way around the tombstones to back of the cemetery, and stood in front of the arch.

"You go first," Adam said.

"You can stay out here," I said.

"But then you'd get the flashlight."

"Yep, I sure would."

"Forget it," he said.

I slipped my hand in my pocket, and wrapped my fingers around the little heart. We stepped inside. I pointed to the last tombstone.

"It's there, in the back," I said.

Adam lit the way with the flashlight.

"Hey, Sammy, is it weird seeing your name on a tombstone?" he asked.

"You have no idea," I said. I emptied my pockets: the candle, the matches, the photo, the heart and the glue.

"You sure this glue will work?" I asked Adam. He'd snitched it from his dad's tool box.

"It says it works on everything, even cement," he said.

I squeezed a drop onto the back of the heart and pressed it against the spot from which the angel had fallen.

"*AAAAHHH!*"

"What! What!" Adam yelped.

"My hand!" I cried.

When I'd touched the tombstone, electricity had zapped through my hand. It burned up my arm, down my shoulder, and into my heart.

"Adam, help," I said. I clutched my chest, but he didn't know what to do.

The voice screamed in my head. "Do you think this will make up for all you've done? Now you will pay! You will feel the same pain I felt for so long!"

"Please stop!" I cried.

"It burns, doesn't it, Sammmanthaaa?" the voice hissed.

My heart felt like it was on fire. The voice in my head laughed so loudly I could hardly hear Adam yelling.

"Sammy, what's happening?"

"Light the candle!" I cried.

Adam reached for the candle and dropped the flashlight. Everything went black.

"Darn it!" he said, fumbling for the candle and the matches.

"Aaahhh!" I wailed. The pain was so intense I couldn't move.

"There you go, Sammmanthaaaa," The voice cooed in my head. "Just like I felt."

Everything around me began spinning. Adam found the candle and lit it. It smelled like mint. The flame flickered and sputtered.

Now my heart was being squeezed as well as burned. I couldn't breathe.

"Adam, the picture. Quick!"

I fell to the ground. I had to fight for every breath. I looked up to see the snake ghost hanging from a branch above me, just as she had before. She had my heart wrapped in her coils.

Each time she moved, my heart felt tighter and tighter!

Chapter Twenty-Six

"My sweeet revvvvenge!" the ghost snake hissed.

A flame shot up in the darkness. Adam had lit the picture.

The snake's eyes went black, as if someone had blown out a candle. Her head rolled back and her coils went limp. She dropped from the tree with a thud.

Adam didn't move. Without the power, he could not see or hear any of it. He held the picture by a corner and watched it burn.

"Is it working, Sammy?" he cried.

He sounded far away. I could hardly open my eyes. But the burning in my chest was going away.

"Sammy, say something! Next, we bury the ashes, right?" Adam was frantic.

"Right," I managed to say. It hurt to talk. It

hurt to move. I was so tired.

"Hang on, Sammy," Adam said, "It's almost over." He dug a little hole with his fingers and scooped the ashes into it.

As he covered the ashes with dirt, vapors rose from the snake's body. They whirled and formed the shape of an old woman in a sweater, her hair pulled into a bun. She looked at me with the saddest eyes I'd ever seen.

"Oh, Nana," I whispered.

"Nana?" Adam asked, swiveling his head in all directions, "You see Nana?"

Poor Nana. I could feel her pain and sadness in my own heart. The ghost lowered her head and sobbed.

I cried too, for Nana, and for my dad. And for my mom. Suddenly, my heart felt empty, as Nadina had said it would.

"Nana," I whispered. "It's going to be all right now. You can rest."

More vapors rose from the ground. They whirled and took the shape of a man dressed in jeans and a T-shirt. He looked at me with gentle eyes.

Dad!

He floated over to Nana and touched her

shoulder. She rested her head on his chest and he held her.

"Oh Adam," I cried, "I wish you could see this."

As I spoke, the vapor of the two ghosts twisted and mingled into a single cloud. Then it was gone.

I felt like I'd just woken from a deep sleep. Adam tried to help me to my feet.

"Can you walk?" he asked.

"I think so," I said, but my feet felt funny, like they weren't touching the ground.

"Good," he said, "because I really want to get out of here."

We walked back to our bikes. I felt strangely light and free. Happy. But Adam was still nervous and scared. I touched his arm.

"It's OK now," I said. "It's really over. The ghost is gone."

I wanted to explain that the snake ghost had really been Nana — her dark side, her pain and anger. And that my dad had appeared, and that it seemed they could rest in peace now because she was finally able to forgive him.

But I knew Adam wouldn't understand until he

heard the whole story about Nana. And I'd promised Aunt Sylvie I wouldn't tell.

Adam and I never told anyone about our night in the graveyard. It was our secret.

The rest of the summer was quiet. Adam and I still fought, but most of the time we got along OK. After a while, I stopped thinking about those first few days I'd had.

Then, on my last night on Bart's Island, as I was getting ready for bed, I noticed a light out in the marsh. A flicker of orange and red.

Uh-oh, I thought. Here we go again.

But there were no raging flames. It just looked like a campfire.

Suddenly, something fluttered in the tree next to the house. A bird darted from behind the leaves, dipped, turned, and flew up to my window. It perched on the sill and cocked its head.

It was the beautiful little jewel bird! He had come, it seemed, to say good-bye.

Then I heard a voice in my head, but it was a man's voice, soft and gentle.

"Samantha," it said. "Tell your mother I love her."

"Dad?"

"Bring her the heart and tell her all is healed."

"But I don't have it. I put it back on Nana's tombstone."

The bird blinked and lifted off the window. He flew toward the marsh and disappeared.

Deep in the marsh, the fire dwindled to a glow. And, soft as the wind, I heard someone crying. A baby! But it wasn't Alfie. It was coming from the marsh.

I pressed my head against the window to listen.

I heard a man and a woman humming a lullaby. It came from the direction of the fire. The crying stopped and turned to a soft cooing sound, like the call of a dove.

I remembered Aunt Sylvie's story, and I smiled. I knew that baby was me.

The night fell silent. The light in the marsh disappeared. I crawled under the covers. I tried to get comfortable, but I felt something hard under my pillow. I lifted the corner, and there it was.

The heart! I turned it around in the palm of my hand. It looked like the same heart, but the crack was gone.

When I got home, I tried to tell Mom all that

had happened, but she had trouble believing me. Who can blame her? Sometimes I don't believe it really happened, either. But whenever I visit a graveyard now, I make sure I don't disturb a thing.

And whenever there's a thunderstorm, you can bet I'll be inside.